FOOTBALL FACTOR
SEEING RED

First published in 2013 by Wayland

Text copyright © Alan Durant 2013
Illustrations © Wayland 2013

Wayland
338 Euston Road
London NW1 3BH

Wayland Australia
Level 17/207 Kent Street
Sydney, NSW 2000

Series Editor: Victoria Brooker
Series design: Robert Walster and Basement68
Cover design: Lisa Peacock
Consultant: Dee Reid

A CIP catalogue record for this book is available
from the British Library.
Dewey number: 823.9'2-dc23

ISBN 978 0 7502 7981 9

2 4 6 8 10 9 7 5 3 1

Printed in China

Wayland is a division of Hachette Children's Books,
an Hachette UK Company
www.hachette.co.uk

FOOTBALL FACTOR

SEEING RED

Alan Durant and Andrew Chiu

WAYLAND
www.waylandbooks.co.uk

"You're off!" shouted the Ref.
He showed Robby the red card.
Robby stormed off the pitch.
His fist still throbbed.

Robby played for Sheldon Rovers.

It was Monday morning.

Dave Brown, Sheldon's manager,

called Robby into his office.

"This has happened too often," said

Dave. "You have one last chance…"

Robby had a three-match ban.
He had to sit in the stands.

Zoltan took his place.

He wasn't as good as Robby.

But he didn't get into fights.

Robby's team, Sheldon Rovers, won.
The next week they drew in the cup.

The third game was a win.
Robby was glum.
"I won't get in the team now,"
he thought.

At training Robby felt bad.

He did not feel part of the team.

"Your ban is over," said the coach,
Joe Ford. "You should be happy."
But Robby wasn't happy at all.

"Come with me," said Joe.

He led Robby to a back room.

There was an old screen.

He told Robby to watch.

It was film of an old game.
One of the teams was Sheldon.
Robby watched a great move.
Then … goal!

The scorer turned with joy.

"Hey, that's you!" Robby said to Joe.

"Yes," Joe nodded. "I was a top striker once. Keep watching."

Sheldon were on the attack again.
Young Joe tried a back flick.
The defender won the ball.

Joe thought it was a foul.

He ran after the defender.

He looked angry.

Joe leapt into the tackle.

Both feet were off the ground.

The defender jumped. Joe slid.

Joe's knee twisted. He cried out.

Joe was in pain.

The ref called for a stretcher.

Joe was carried off.

The ref showed him a red card.

"No more football for me," said Joe. "One stupid moment. It finished everything."

Robby didn't know what to say.

Joe looked hard at Robby.

"Just don't do what I did," he said.

"Walk away from trouble. Let your
skill do the talking."

Saturday was the Cup replay.

Robby was on the bench.

It was 1–1.

There were twenty minutes left.

The manager sent Robby on.

Robby got the ball from Kyle.

He was about to shoot when…

Agh! His legs were taken. He fell.

Robby saw red.

His hand balled into a fist.

Then he thought of Joe.
He shook the player's hand.

The game was nearly over.
Robby got a free kick. He took it.
The ball bent round the wall…

… into the top corner of the net.

"Goal!"

Robby turned to Joe and grinned.
His skills had done the talking.

Robby's team-mates jumped on him.
The only red he saw was their shirts.
Robby had won the game for Sheldon!

Read more stories about Sheldon Rovers.

Sheldon Rovers have made it to the Cup final. It is their manager Dave Brown's last match. Will Danny, Robby, Naz, Ledley and Tom play their best? Can they make Dave's day and win the Cup?

Danny is playing his first match for Sheldon Rovers. It is the first round of the Cup. He needs to play well to keep his place. But will nerves get the better of him?

Naz is Sheldon Rover's top scorer. He is a goal machine. But suddenly things start to go wrong. He can't score at all. He loses his place in the team. Will he ever get his goal touch back?

Tom plays in goal for Sheldon Rovers. He has a lucky horseshoe that he takes to every match. But on Cup semi-final day it goes missing. Things start to go wrong. Has Tom's luck run out?

Robby keeps getting sent off. Now he has got a three-match ban and he feels down. Can he learn to control his temper? Will he ever get back in the team?

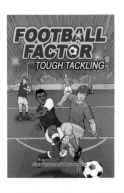

Ledley is a defender for Sheldon Rovers. He has been out injured for months. His first game is the Cup quarter final. Will he last the game? Will his tackling be strong enough?

FOR TEACHERS

About Freestylers

Freestylers is a series of carefully levelled stories, especially geared for struggling readers of both sexes. With very low reading age and high interest age, these books are humorous, fun, up-to-the-minute and edgy. Core characters provide familiarity in all of the stories, build confidence and ease pupils from one story through to the next, accelerating reading progress.

Freestylers can be used for both guided and independent reading. To make the most of the books you can:

- Focus on making each reading session successful. Talk about the text before the pupil starts reading. Introduce the characters, the storyline and any unfamiliar vocabulary.

- Encourage the pupil to talk about the book during reading and after reading. How would they have felt if they were one of the characters playing for Sheldon Rovers? How would they have dealt with the situations that the players found themselves in?

- Talk about which parts of the story they like best and why.

For guidance, this story has been approximately measured to:

National Curriculum Level: 1B
Reading Age: 6
Book Band: Orange

ATOS: 1.2
Lexile ® Measure [confirmed]: 150L